The Man Who Loved Literature

CUPPA CLASSICS

The Man Who Loved Literature

Guram Dochanashvili

THE BROWSER

Title: The Man Who Loved Literature
Author: Guram Dochanashvili

ISBN: 978-93-49042-09-4
Imprint: The Browser | Cuppa Classics

Published by:
JGS Enterprises Pvt Ltd
SCO 14-15, FF, Sector 8-C,
Chandigarh 160 009
Website: cuppaclassics.com
Email: service@thebrowser.org

First published in 2001
This edition is published by The Browser in 2025
Printed in India

cuppa cappuccino classics | THE BROWSER

Contents

The Man Who Loved Literature

What we present below is one of the very popular short stories by the Georgian prose-writer Guram Dochanashvili.

The writer's style (even in translation, we hope) displays a light touch, brilliance and humour which seldom fail to appeal to readers. It is difficult to imagine Georgian prose, Georgian cinema, or putting it another way, the Georgian way of thinking, without humour. And it is always individual, it always (in terms of creative work) helps reveal underlying human attitudes to the surrounding world.

Guram Dochanashvili was born in Tbilisi in 1939. He published his first collected stories at the age of 27, before that finishing a music school in the violin class, graduating from the History Department at Tbilisi University, and working for several years at the History. Archaeology and Ethnography Institute (archaeology, Stone Age). At the time Guram Dochanashvili published his first work, the generation of Georgian writers of the 1960s had practically been formed. This generation appeared at the turn of the 1960s and the most brilliant figure was Nodar Dumbadze whose works have been published in the journal (see "Soviet Literature" No. 10, 1976, No. 1, 1981, No. 12, 1982, No. 9. 1083)

This generation was marked by an inspired assertion of intransient human values, persistent rejection of evil, and unflinching faith that good would triumph. With its folk, national elements, humour proved, in the final count, to be a reflection of the same inspiration, furiously accepting or rejecting certain ways of living and certain attitudes to life.

"The Man Who Loved Literature" has been produced on radio and TV and staged in the theatre. It has been translated into other languages

Guram Dochanashvili works a great deal in the cinema, as do many writers in contemporary Georgia. Recently, he has assumed the extensive responsibilities of chief editor of the Georgia Film Studios.

Georgian literature has traditionally had excellent short stories with a large range of meanings. But are there many short-story writers with-out an urge to write novels? Guram Dochanashvili has also written his novel, ("Three Gifts"): the hero of the novel wanders through the world, the subject, time and place of action are to a large extent symbolic. Only one thing is quite definite: the search by the hero and the writer of high moral truths. And despite the exotic in Dochanashvili's writing, in the end the reader will discover what is truly important in the prose of this purposeful Georgian author.

ALEXANDER RUDENKO-DESNYAK

Chapter I

It all began with my chief sending for me.

"Our future investigation," he said, "shall concern social aspects of the everyday behaviour of blue-collar and white-col-lar workers inhabiting settlements of an urban type, and determine its dependence on the conditions of their lives. In the study of leisure-time occupations to which today considerably more attention is paid than was the case previously, the behaviour and actions of an individual in the non-production sphere occupy no insignificant place—Er, got a match?"

Unfortunately I had none.

"On the one hand," he continued, "scientific and technical progress and the improvement in living conditions which accompanies it at the contemporary stage..."

"I'll go out and get some—"

"No need, I want to stop smoking, anyway.... In the use of time outside the production process the daily occupation of an individual becomes an increasingly important element of his life; therefore, first, special attention should be paid to his leasure occupations, this being one of the factors in the formation of personality, and a component in the delineation of life and behaviour; second, research of such a nature enables us to determine the most effective mechanism for influencing the consciousness of the individual; and third, this sphere has been studied less than any other equally important factor of economic and social development."

He paused for a moment and I put in an understanding "Yes."

"The study of the leisure problem from that angle," my chief continued, "is very topical, and its elaboration is of both the-oretical and practical interest. As a theme planned for one year it is, obviously, too extensive. We shall, therefore, present the question in the following manner: you will study the employment of daily non-production time and its dependence on the conditions of life, limiting your selection of subjects to one trade or profession, the choice being left to you. Is that clear?"

"Quite"

"With regard to the questions which you will put to persons of the trade or profession you select, in other words the respondents, they are here—five pages of them. The replies should be expressive, brief and exhaustive."

"Simultaneously?"

"Naturally. If you come up against something unclear or complicated, you can always turn to me—in working hours.... You heard the defence of the yesterday's thesis?"

"Yes"

"How did it go?"

"All right, just as usual."

"Many people?"

"Oh—some."

"Were there many criticisms?"

"No, not really. This and that."

"Yes—I almost forgot," my chief suddenly recalled. "It is absolutely essential to make especial note of the way in which the material and economic factor affects one or another form of leisure occupation."

II

That evening I looked through the questionnaire; the questions were clear, simple and at the same time interesting. I do enjoy my job, or to be more exact, I enjoy putting questions to strangers, you find yourself in a new state, mood and particularly new stage of dynamism, and purposefulness—all taken together. One individual likes one thing, a second something else and a third something different again; you write and write and something is achieved.

However, the following day—morning, to be exact—I encountered my first difficulty, the choice of my respondents' profession. A factory would be noisy and besides, people who are tired would not give an exhaustive reply; shop assistants have no time and anyway, they can't leave their customers who constantly demand service, and I could hardly chase them home. Truck drivers don't want to lose precious time just because of me and doctors and nurses are out of the question, they can have a twenty-four stretch of duty; what I wanted was people whose jobs began and ended at a definite time. So I racked my brains until my eyes brought me my answer when they came to rest on photographer's studio in a quiet street. The very thing! Photographers are usually lively and talkative, they would find plenty of time for exhaustive answers to my questions while awaiting their elaborately coiffed clients. Besides, they have a sober view of life through the accurate lens of their cameras. So I energetically pushed onen the door, said "Good morning" and heard the polite response. "Are you free?" I asked. "Why else am I sitting here?" However, on learning the purpose of my visit he seemed somewhat taken aback; he looked me up and down, while I tried to appear pleasant and sincere, straightened my tie and smiled a sincere smile; but he, head bent sideways, continued to subject to a close scrutiny this stranger who was interested in his leisure occupations. To prevent him from complicating matters with the fully reasonable query: "What business is it of yours?" I hastened to explain that that I was an emissary from such a competent organisation as ours is, sent to inquire of people in his profession how they spend their leisure time, whether they like the cinema, sport, the TV, about their family status, their living conditions and so on and so forth; once only when some rather ambiguous expression like "institutions" and "organs" slipped out, something in his face twitched; I at once altered my choice of vocabularly (very important in such cases) and explained în ordinary simple words that the questionnaire enabled us investigators to learn the wishes of people in various professions, become acquainted with their views, all of which would help us where possible to improve their lives and raise their standard of living; at that he changed, gave a sigh of relief and let out a heartfelt "Thank heaven!"

We talked frankly, cordially, surrounded by photographs of handsome self-satisfied women; my respondent replied with laconic expressiveness. I made a few jokes, he laughed, and I straightened my tie. I like to fuss with my tie, probably because its presence fusses me; however, for our job a tie is a "must", at least I regard it as such; my respondent considered light music better than the classical kind, sports broadcasts better than interviews with agricultural workers, thought it no great pleasure to stand in a long queue, and found it vastly preferable to sit by the window of a half-empty bus and seek the lucky numbers on private cars rather than to stand on tip-toe, jammed in a tram packed to suffocation. Within some fifteen minutes the questionnaire was filled according to all the rules, and in addition we had exchanged some amusing stories—mine were better. Filling in the second questionnaire at a photographer's two or three blocks away, by the public garden was even easier because my first respondent had taken a fancy to me and gave me a note to his colleague: "Misha, man the bringing this note is a good guy, one of our sort." The third questionnaire, which I filled with brief replies from a photographer half-dead with boredom, came out quite satisfactory. I then went to my chief.

"How is your work going?" he asked. "Excellently," I said, "I've already got some filled." "No, not really!" he said and patted my shoulder approvingly. How splendid it is when your chief is young, healthy and strong, a real athlete, and at the same time has a moderate acquaintance with fashion, wearing side-whiskers just a mite lengthened, a jacket very slightly shaped at the waist, square-heeled shoes and a handkerchief in his breast pocket matching his tie. He ran his eye over my questionnaires. "Very good, very good work you've done, only—this graph, public utilities, would be improved if it were not just given under two headings, good and bad, as you have done, but with another three added. First, provision of all types of utilities such as running water, drains, central heating, gas, bath or shower and hot water. Second, provision of the basic utilities—running water, drainage and central heating and third—minus drains. But taken generally, you've done well, carry on the same way. How are things at home, everything all right?" He went on talking for a few moments in the same vein, cordial and friendly, in an excellent mood, but suddenly remembered something, I don't know what, turned thoughtful, then put on his dark glasses, rested his chin on his chest and concluded curtly.

"As I have already said, the employment of leisure time is characterised by two groups of indices: a) the list of occupations and b) data on the prolongation, intensity and similar qualitative parameters of such occupations."

III

It had all begun well enough, but the next morning, Thursday, I collided with the individual who spoiled it all—collided?—it was I myself, on my own two feet who entered that damned studio. He didn't even hear me, he was gazing at something, the devil alone knows what, in the far distance. He was leaning forward, resting his elbows on the glass-covered table and staring right through me at that distant something, as though I too were made of glass; his eyes glittered and I had an instant foreboding that this one meant trouble. However, I coughed; he started and smiled with some embarrassment.

"Certainly, certainly—do you want a passport photo or—"

I began a detalled explanation; he listened attentively, he evidently understood everything but after a moment he interrupted.

"Excuse me—have you come on your own initative, or—"

He stopped, then added, "Lord, but you do remind me of somebody!"

"No, my chief sent me."

"Excuse me, but I need to know who he is, that chief, the sort of person.... No, who is it you remind me of?"

"What—you want me to bring my chief here?" I joked, although I already felt some irritation.

"No, of course not, what need for that? Describe him in a few words so I can get some idea of the person I actually have to do with."

"Well, how shall I put it? He's young, determined, energetic, modern. Although he's young, some of the junior employees have been assigned to him for guidance and he's already made an excellent beginning with them." "An excellent beginning?"

"Yes!" A gust of anger rose in me. "An excellent beginning!"

"M'yes," he said, sounding rather sad. "And Marshal Edmondo Betancourt made an excellent beginning, but how he ended is well known."

"Marshal—who?"

"Why, Marshal Betancourt, of course, not Aureliano the Fat!" He suddenly slapped his forehead. "Oh—why didn't I see it at once! You're amazingly like Aureliano the Fat-before he got so fat, of course. Just think," he marvelled, "such a likeness!"

"Who on earth is that fatty you're talking about?"

"Why, the son of the Marshal's cousin, the one Diego incarcerated.... You remember? Eulali's husband. H'm! I picture him in his youth, before he got fat—exactly like you are now, an amazing likeness! And there was me, thinking I'd met you somewhere." Then—just imagine!—he asked me, "Can you explain it?"

His eyes held a lively spark. Is he deranged, flashed through my mind, but if he were, he wouldn't be kept on the job.

"Aren't you ashamed—to come to work when you've been drinking?"

"What, me—drunk?" he snapped back, then suddenly his face took on a reproving expression. "A-ah, I understand, you haven't read the novel about Betancourt—you haven't, have you?"

"No, I haven't. Perhaps you'd be so good as to answer my questions!"

"With pleasure, with pleasure. And the novel about Anselmo, too, and Llosa, Mario Vargas—?"

"No."

"And Cortazar?"

"No."

I thought he was pulling my leg but he looked at me enviously.

"You're a fortunate man."

"Why?"

"Because such a great pleasure is still before you. With me, it's already behind, alas!"

"What pleasure?"

"The pleasure of reading all this for the first time. It seems, South Ameri—"

"Excuse me." I couldn't stand it any more. "Unless I'm badly mistaken, you're the respondent, not me."

"And just what is a respondent?"

"The one to whom questions are put."

"Ah, and for you the prefix 'co' is added, right? At the beginning of the word—'co-respondent'."

"No, I'm the interviewer."

"All right, my dear fellow, let's have your questions." But at that moment the door was hesitatingly pushed slightly open and a shy-looking individual edged into the studio. My respondent with an apology turned his attention to the client—invited him to remove his outer things, seated him, lifted his head with a touch on the chin and turned it from side to side, borrowed my tie and fixed it on him, turned on a brilliant light, told the man to raise his head, said "Quiet!" and removed something from the lens. With a word of thanks he returned my tie, having first awkwardly loosed the knot, which left me unable to put it on again as I cannot tie it—I always get my brother to do it in the mornings; the respondent, downcast, said, "Oh, I am sorry, and I don't know how either," and turned back to the client. "No, it won't be ready tomorrow, come the day after." He pocketed the money—eighty kopecks, handed over a receipt with a smile, said "Good morning" and turned back to me, every line of him expressing attention.

"Excuse me, but it's working hours, you know."

With the back of my hand I moved the tie off the questionnaire and began.

"Your surname?"

"Kezheradze."

"Given name?"

"Vasiko"

"Vasili, that is?"

"Yes, of course. The 'ko' you can give or not—your privelege as correspondent."

"I've told you already, I'm not a newspaper correspondent." Very distinctly I concluded, "I'm an *interviewer*, get me?—Year of birth, please."

"Twenty-nine."

"Nineteen hundred—?"

"Naturally."

"Sex?"

"I am called Vasili," he answered, copying my tone. I wrote "Male."

"Profession?"

"Specialist in photography."

I got down to the main points.

"Do you like your work?"

Somewhat reluctantly he said, "More or less."

"Why is that?"

He gave me an attentive, rather melancholy look and answered obliquely, "I'm very fond of literature."

There was a pause, then I asked, "Specialised?"

He smiled. "No, fiction."

I was a little at a loss but took care not to show it.

"Splendid," I said. "We'll be talking about literature, one of the questions touches upon it."

"No, no-o," and again he was smiling. "Not just 'touching upon it', we'll be beginning and ending with it."

"What?!"

"What?—in your questions to respondents like me."

"How do you know?" I was getting definitely annoyed. "At present I intend to find out what utilities there are in your house, what are your living conditions—very good, bad or moderately good. What has literature to do with that, especially taken narrowly—fiction!"

"Oh no, you're out there." He smiled teasingly and unceremoniously looked down at my questionnaire. "I may not have any central heating but all the same my living conditions are excellent—call them utilities or whatever pleases you."

"What do you mean?"

"That I have two huge bookcases and bookshelves, all well filled, a comfortable armchair and a wall lamp over my head when I sit there."

"But those aren't utilities."

"Depends on who has them." With a touch of irony he added, "So you regard fiction as literature in a narrow sense?"

"Of course, because literature can also be documentary, scientific, popular, textbook—"

"You're forgetting pamphlets, my friend."

"Yes, those too." I wasn't letting myself be put off, the important thing is to stick to what you're after, so I continued. "Do you like the cinema?"

"No."

"Why not?"

"The cinema is a financed competitor."

"Whose?"

"I told you, I don't like it, it doesn't feed the brain so much as please the eye, that's why."

I wrote "No", but after that I felt silly putting the next question: "What films do you prefer?"

But he answered, "Those with captions, obviously."

Oho, so he could become irritated, too.

I was seething, but another client appeared and the man who loved literature could not contain himself and vented his annoyance on the innocent newcomer. "Sit down, sit down, don't take all day!" and switched on such a strong light that the lamps hummed. He jerked the client's head with a grip on his chin, but then cooled down and stroked his hair—"Excuse me, you have nothing to do with my irritation. Your hair is a bit disordered." The client, somewhat taken aback, smiled broadly, and my respondent smiled back, the seated one remained frozen in immobility, while the other fussed by the camera. Then he said, "Quiet!" He helped the client on with his coat although the latter continued to smile as he repeated, "No, it's all right. I can manage—" and when the door had closed behind him it was my turn to be taken aback—it was a completely different man who was regarding me with a challenging, contemptuous look.

"We can postpone the rest until tomorrow if you like," I suggested.

"No, no need, let's have your questions."

I selected a question which, I thought, could not possibly have any connection with his love of literature.

"What do you think of the fashions? What sort of clothes do your prefer?"

The answer was prompt.

"The ones with broad pockets, the rest doesn't matter."

"With—broad pockets? What's that for?"

"So that they'll—hold any size book."

The man was evidently a bit touched. I rose.

"Excuse me, but my chief's expecting me."

"Determined and energetic, eh? Well, can't be helped. Goodbye."

He watched me, dissatisfied, as I slipped my pen into my breast pocket and the questionnaire into my brief-case, and as I turned towards the door he spoke again "You've forgotten something."

The "something" was my tie.

"Oh—thanks. Goodbye," and carefully, trying not to crease it, I pushed the tie into my pocket.

"But you'll be coming again, you know."

"Never!" burst from me. I'd wasted àlid hour on him.

"We'll see."

"Where d'you get that idea?"

"We can't part for good without getting to know one another properly, so far our talk has been more suitable for a humourous magazine."

"And we're not likely to come up with anything better," I retorted.

"Why not? It all lies ahead. We'll be talking again—you'll see."

"I certainly don't intend to set a foot inside here again,"

"We'll see." He smiled.

I went out in the worst of tempers, with sweat running down my forehead. I fumbled in my pocket for a handkerchief and wiped my face, then felt something wrong in what I was holding.

It was my tie.

IV

My chief was wearing a sweater, beautifully hand-knitted, moulded to his strong, muscular body—women went crazy over him—some of them, anyway. A real athlete! A scientist, and such a powerful torso! And his speech was weighty, convincing, full of complex, meticulously exact terms—he seemed to know them all, a walking dictionary of foreign words! There was one thing that surprised me, though—although he had such handsome eyes and brows, he liked to wear dark glasses. He was wearing them now, sitting in his armchair, reading my questionnaire with occasional murmurs of "Interesting, interesting." I was delighted, fidgetting on my seat; he was reading the last questionnaire, in a moment he would praise me.... Incidentally, I have one peculiarity, if I am worried and anxious. I get fearfully sleepy. The first few times it happened I thought it was just chance, but later, when I found it constantly repeated, I took my trouble to a famous specialist; he read my letter of recommendation, examined me, said that he could find nothing dangerous, similar cases were known in the history of medicine, and it was noteworthy that sleepiness came only with the foreboding of unpleasantness; pleasant excitement such as the present expectation of praise brought no sleepiness. I said nothing to the people I worked with about my strange peculiarity, they wouldn't believe me or understand—or else it wouldn't take long for them to start tapping their foreheads.

My chief smiled at me "You've worked well. Good man." A brief phrase, but all of it pleasant—"worked well, good man." "When did you manage to get all this done, eh?" I smiled and dropped my eyes modestly; he laid his hand on my shoulder and continued. "An excellent beginning. The words were familiar, where had I heard them—someone had said them quite recently, yes, it was that daft fellow who had spoken about some Edmondo who had begun excellently, but had ended—! "There ought to have been one more questionnaire filled in," I said, "but it was quite impossible to get anywhere with that ass." "So you gave it up?" "Yes" I said rather uncertainly, but my chief said. "You did the right thing, if the respondent doesn't want to cooperate best leave him alone and find another. There are enough of them!" "He really was very strange." My effervescence had rather subsided but I tried to smile. "He judged everything from the viewpoint of literature—narrowly understood, fiction." "From the viewpoint of literature?" repeated my chief, mildly interested. "How did he do that?" "Well, it was like this." I recalled. "He began by saying that he had excellent utilities because he had two book cases and bookshelves well filled and a convenient light." My chief laughed heartily. "So he didn't know what utilities are! What else?" "What else—" I flogged my memory again. "Yes—I spoke about fashion, asked him what kind of clothes he liked, and he said the main thing was that they should have broad pockets so that any book could go in—just imagine!" "No—really?" said my chief, then rose and went to the window where he stood, thoughtfully gazing out into the street. Without turning, he continued, "That's rather interesting. What else did he say?" "Nothing, I got up and left." "Get up and go—there's always time for that; but the questionnaire should have been filled first. Or perhaps he didn't want to answer any more?" "Nothing like that," I confessed. "In fact, he said we'd be meeting again." "He was right!" Just think, that was what he said. "And I'll tell you why." He walked up and down the room, back and forth, while I stood looking at him. "He was right"—what did he have in mind when he said that? And a foreboding of something unpleasant brought the usual attack of sleepiness, but at that moment I recalled something else. "Oh, yes, and I asked him what films he liked, and he said those with captions."

"Why?" "I suppose it's because you have to read them." "He loves reading to such an extent? Oho!" My chief rubbed his hands. "We mustn't let this sample slip away from us!" Again he paced the floor. "Just think!" He gazed meditatively, and suddenly rounded on me with a hall of questions. "Do you consider that the unusual replies of an individual who accepts the whole complex of questions only from the viewpoint of his chosen occupation isn't preferable to one who mouths a collection of cliches? You assume that you can treat fiction with contempt, wave it aside? Don't you find it pleasant to sit in the shade reading, say, Dickens? Isn't reading one of the best forms of cultural recreation?" My chief paused and I could sense that his thoughts had turned to his own future work—it is at these times that he throws back his head, bent a little sideways, and in that moment becomes inimitable, unbending. Even behind his dark glasses I could see his stern, piercing eyes, and suddenly—just imagine!—he sharply ordered me, "Be so good as to go at once, today, to the respondent in question and fill in the questionnaire with his answers, taking his wishes into consideration, and remember that a few statements by unusual individuals can be of far greater interest than the hackneyed answers of a dozen commonplace ones. However, first I must make sure that this man really has an extraordinary love of books, of reading—as one of the forms of cultural occupation; and then, if fiction really does run like a red thread through his whole life, we should discover the reason." In a somewhat softer tone he concluded, "Well, run along. Go and work on him."

V

My legs carried me there reluctantly, but there was nothing else I could do. I had to go back to the man crazed over literature. The street ran downhill and was covered with a film of ice into the bargain, but for the thick layer of sawdust which had been sprinkled about, walking would have been impossible. All the same I stepped cautiously. And raged. Who was I going to, and what the devil did I want with him! I was in a wretched mood and when some woman slipped I felt better, I even smiled, but finding myself beside the familiar studio my nervous irritation returned and I began to yawn. The light was on; I took a deep breath, pushed the door open and stopped short, confused. Nobody to be seen. I stood there, puzzled, until I heard a muffled voice. "I'll be out in a minute, I'm just doing some prints!" I looked round and discovered the narrow door the voice had come from, so I sat down and prepared to wait. Now, it is far from pleasant, waiting for somebody you don't want to see. I began looking round the walls; nearly all the photographs were looking directly at me, only one or two heads were turned away or drooping languorously sideways; I found the insistent stare of a bespectacled child especially unpleasant and turned my attention to a personage in a deep *décolleté* but she, with assumed indifference, looked past me. At any moment my respondent would enter and my nerves were jumping. My agitation increased, it was worse and worse.... The charming lady is now looking in my direction but I have no attention to spare for her, I am weak, I am heavy heavier.... "Let me alone," I say or think, I no longer know which. I am limp, weak, but she does not need, she lays a hand tenderly on my shoulder, whispering stealthily "Iano, iano—"

"No, no," I say or think and collapse, melting, but the hand is still on my shoulder and I hear the same stealthy voice, "Liano, liano." Let me alone. I don't want anything else, only let me alone, don't disturb me, wait.... A trolleybus rushes past on the rain-wet asphalt, the tires rustle, but she continues, stealthily and teasingly, with her "Reliano, reliano" and claps her hands. I open my eyes, I love applause, I photograph her myself, but she parts into two, dissolves into a violet focus but I hear clearly, "Ureliano, ureliano..." and see clearly, with my waking eyes, that this is no lady, it's my respondent! I fell asleep, it seems, and he was shaking my shoulder to waken me. "Aureliano! I told you that you'd be back, you'd come again, Aureliano!"

VI

It's no good, try as I will, I cannot overcome my annoying habit; whether I want or not, the anticipation of something unpleasant makes me sleepy and if nothing prevents it finally sends me off. However, I didn't lose my head, I rose with an apologetic explanation. "I was working late last night, looking at books till dawn." "What kind—fiction?" He was on his hobby-horse again, but this time it just suited me and, fully awake now, remembering my chief's instructions, I suggested, "Shall we continue?—The questions." He agreed at once, "Of course, of course." Turning to the narrow door he said, "You prepare the hypo, Klim." "Who's Klim?" I asked. "My assistant." I opened my briefcase, laid the questionnaire on the table, cautiously pressed the pen against my finger (it leaks) and put my first question.

"Do you feel much of your time is wasted?"

"None at all."

That surprised me. "How is that?"

Surprised in his turn, he asked, "Why should I want to waste time?"

"You misunderstand me," I explained courteously. "Naturally you don't wish to waste your time, but you have to use public transport, or shops, you have to make your supper or go to a canteen for din—"

"On the contrary, it's you who haven't understood. I actually do not waste time, when I'm standing in a queue, or frying an egg, or travelling in a tram."

"How do you manage that?" I was feeling some irritation again.

"Simple! Do you think a love of literature means only reading? Don't you need to think about what you've read? What difference does it make whether you sit or a term, you can think in any position, even doing a handstand."

"All right, but what do you think about?"

"What I've just been reading. Or what I remember."

Ugh, I could have wished my chief to the.... But all the same, I continued.

"And if you're out of humour?"

"Oh, that's just the time when you need to think—when you're out of humour."

"Why?"

"So as to bring yourself back into a good mood."

Crazy. Some sort of maniac. And he kept staring at me, and marvelling. "Lordy, but how like you are to Aurelians the Fat. I say, you don't mind if I call you Aureliano?"

The liberties he took!

"Be so good as to keep to the rules of etiquette," I said loftily. "My name is Tamaz."

He spread his palms slightly and his whole form expressed submission.

"Very well, Tamaz, very well, my dear fellow."

I looked away.

"A human being has one surprising attribute," he said thoughtfully without any kind of introduction, and I saw he had changed completely, his eyes had lost their sly sparkle; it was another man who faced me, sombre, withdrawn into himself.

After a moment's deep thought he looked at me and told me something incredible about—what do you think?—About toads! It appears that a toad sees an insect caly when it is moving, it flies past and the toad makes for it, but if no insect moves nearby the toad's eyes are covered by a grey film; that, it appears, is because its brain is extremely primitive, if the load saw everything round it, all the colours, its brain could not stand the strain and it would die.

"But a human being," he continued, "a human brain—it's quite different, a human being becomes dull, slow-witted if he doesn't think, doesn't see, take anything in, dream and plan. So standing in a queue doesn't necessarily mean wasting time, stand and think, who's going to stop you. Whether you want it or not, there is always something to see or hear. You don't believe me? Shut your eyes, that's right. Well, can you see?"

"Of course not."

"What about hearing?"

"No."

"Listen. Listen hard."

Something was dripping somewhere. There was the distant sound of a car.

"Now do you hear anything?"

"Yes"

"And even if you cover your ears, all the same you'll imagine something because that's how a man is made. Try it."

Interested, I shut my eyes and covered my ears. At first there was nothing but coloured spots that danced against the blackness, and just to spite my respondent I tried not to imagine anything, but suddenly a camera on a crooked tripod rose before me, and when I opened my eyes I started in surprise. A very small, scraggy youth of eighteen or maybe twenty, hair parted at the side, insignificant but quick, was vigorously brushing his stained sleeve with a brush. I stared, bewildered—where on earth had he sprung from? But my respondent said, "My assistant, Klim."

Of course—I should have guessed; the narrow door was open, I had been sitting with eyes shut and ears covered, naturally I hadn't noticed him come in.

"Pleased to meet you," said Klim cheerfully and held out his small hand. I held out mine, he took it, then looked at my fingers. "Is your fountain pen leaking? Show it to me." I did so. He turned it about, frowning, then briskly took a little bottle from a drawer, opened it, anointed the pen with a yellow liquid, blew on it, turned it around and returned it to me.

"Here you are, it'll be all right now."

The respondent noted it, well satisfied.

"A real handy lad, that, gets things fixed in no time." He turned back to me. "Did you see anything?"

"When?"

"When your eyes were shut."

"Yes, a camera."

"There, you see, you even remembered the camera." His eyes became thoughtful again. "And how many novels much more interesting than any apparatus you could have read, for instance—oh, so many there are—which shall we ask him about, Klim?"

"*Madame Bovary*" Klim breathed reverently.

"Yes,—have you read *Madame Bovary*?"

"Er—no," I said with an effort, and looking straight at me he continued, "Will you believe me sincere if I express admiration?"

"No."

"Well, then we'd better say nothing."

Even Klim, a kid not yet dry behind the ears, looked at me reprovingly; I seldom blush but I felt my colour rising.

"I'll make a point of reading it."

"Oho," said the respondent, laying his hand on my shoulder, and changed in a moment, smiling kindly at me. He seemed to have been pleased with me.

VII

He had an urgent job, printing the photograph of some power engineering specialists who had graduated ten years before, so we went through the narrow doorway and continued our talk in the red semi-darkness as he made his prints. His replies were brief, clear and calm, so I took advantage of the moment to put the question which nobody as a rule could answer quickly. "Are you satisfied with your life?" He, however, said at once. "That depends upon the author I meet on the day in question." While we talked, somebody's eyebrows, lips, eyes, hair would appear on the white paper lying in the bath. "Like being born," my respondent joked. "Sometimes you get such interesting faces—like yours, excuse me, but you are so like Aureliano before he got fat, a real copy of him, Tamaz. This one," and he touched the "newly-born" with his tweezers, "he looks a harmless sort of fellow, but you'd never believe the bad-tempered mugs we get sometimes, and the conceited, self-satisfied ones. But of course there are plenty of good-natured, friendly-looking ones.... What—do I address meeting? No—in the first place they don't often get us photographers together for meetings, but even if they had them every day I wouldn't get up to speak. I can't say the same thing to people with differing levels of knowledge, differing ways; how can one say the same thing to two people, one of whom has never read, for instance—Klim, one of the great writers—yes, who has never read Stendahl, say, and the other knows him nearly by heart. How can you possibly talk the same way with them?—Klim, I think we'll print this now. As for your next question, which science attracts me most—hard to say. I'm weak on the sciences. Perhaps I should start by saying what *I don't like*; Well, say—mathematics. Heavens, Klim, what a face, the smug self-satisfaction of it!" Looking at the wet print, he went on, "What can he be worth! I'd like to know who he is, what he's like at work, and at home with his family. Klim, make another print, we'll hang him in the studio, in the most prominent place, everyone looking at him will understand how disgusting extreme self-satisfaction is. Yes, I was talking about mathematics. It's called an exact science, but it's very far from always being that. I'll give you one example: there's a man I know, I've known him since he was a kid, from his earliest years he had everything he wanted, he was cosseted and spoiled, poor fellow, and that was how he grew up, but even then his parents still gave him everything he wanted, and the unfortunate fellow was always dissatisfied, always fed up with life; right up to this very day he has the face of a hungry man just because he is always full-fed; and if that is the case how can you experience the pleasure of being satisfied? So do you know what he thought up, what idea his empty mind concocted? He decided to show himself satisfied, he assumed a self-satisfied expression, just like that one you see in the photograph."

Klim had been listening attentively; suddenly he exclaimed in chagrin, "Oh, damn it, I've kept it in too long, it's nearly black."

The face on the photo really did look as though it had been blacked with charcoal, but the lover of books only said, "That's no tragedy, Klim, we've plenty more paper!" "Plenty of paper, that's right. But all the same I shouldn't have left it in." My respondent, however, recognising in the spoiled photo that same self-satisfied individual, said contemptuously, "No great loss—one would think he'd been a professor and you'd blackened the original!" Turning back to me, "Well, then, mathematics. Say, this specimen spoiled with having too much of everything, self-satisfied, is standing in the street and alongside him—Klim, tell me the name of one of the great writers—the really great.... Oh, you couldn't find a better! Well, the great Spaniard is standing beside him, proud, ragged, a hungry cripple, and our luxurious self-satisfied blockhead, my acquaintance, that wretched no-good I've just told you about—it doesn't matter that they lived in different periods, there were plenty of them at that time, too. Well, say they are standing side by side—it's perfectly all right to go back in thought through the centuries—and a mathematician of that day passes, average or a genius doesn't matter, and if you ask him how many people there are in the street and he says 'Two—' will that be correct, I ask you? *This* and *that* make two? One plus one, eh? No, no, there are times when mathematics is not an exact science; but in literature, my friend, such inexactitude is ruled out although it is of all sciences the most lawless. The world 'lawless' in this case does not at all have its usual meaning. Nobody can say that once two riders travelled in Spain, one tall and thin, hurrying, knowing no peace, and the other, short and fat, following after him.... Take it out, Klim, take it out—what, again it's black? What's the matter with you?" he laughed.

We stood talking in the dim light and I gradually filled in the questionnaire.

"Have I a family? No, none, I did have a girl-friend once, and after her I just couldn't marry. I sometimes go around with women, the usual thing, nothing to hide about it, but marry—no, I'll never marry. You want to know why? I'll try to explain. We loved each other so much.... She could have left me for anyone you like, anyone—a rickety, ugly intellectual, or a peasant with gnarled hands, a musician or a worker, even a physicist-lyricist—one gets mix-ups like that, too, these days, although I've never understood what there is in common between physics and lyrics except the endings, they make a good rhyme—but no, she left me for the kind who nauseates me like none other, a mass of fat self-satisfaction.... I passed them in the street one day, my former fiancée, beautiful with her mysterious inscrutable beauty like the words 'lapis lazuli', and beside her a man with that disgustingly smug, self-satisfied look—like the word 'gluttonous', and I stood on one side, superfluous, like the word 'in order to'. Oh.... take it out, Klim, take it out, yes, at last it's just right."

So we stood there, talking.

VIII

My chief looked at me seriously, he even took off his glasses to fix me better with his eyes. I had summed up the main character of the questionnaire: the answer to every question was linked with fiction; my chief listened, then his thoughts would obviously fly to his own future scientific work, he would throw back his head with a slight bend sideways and raising one eyebrow, look away into an unimaginable distance, now and then exclaiming, "Aha.... Aha.... Good, good!" I gave a detailed explanation of the replies I had written down—the respondent did not like mathematics because the writer Cervantes plus some bit of insignificance did not make up the number two, that is, one plus one, that the said respondent had lost his fiancée to a man as repulsive as the word "gluttonous", that he never wasted a second because in a crowded tram he could think about literature—but only in the narrow meaning of the word, I added, only fiction. I presented my chief with everything in order; from time to time he would listen keenly as we noted facts. "So he doesn't waste time, then?" he said in a hushed, mysterious voice. "Yes, he assured me that he doesn't." "That's excellent, splendid. Now that's the kind of thing I understand, an individual. But you, do you realise what we've found? A parametrically intelligibly expressed individual capable of answering questions which concern much more significant spheres; and can you possibly wave off fiction as such? Wasn't fiction served by the pen of Leo Tolstoy, of Herzen, er—a whole series of famous writers? All right, that's enough," my chief concluded. "Let's go, this respondent is a real find, just made for complex questions." He was actually a bit excited! "We'll go to him—if only we find him in." "We'll find him in all right, where else could he be but—" "Right, then come along," he cut me off sharply.

We marched along the street side by side, my chief and I, and although he was excited still he stepped firmly, confidently; his coat sat well on his athletic form, his hair was springy, his gaze piercing, there was something of the eagle about him—strong, bold. It felt good to be walking with him like this, side by side, shoulder to shoulder like equals, I hoped we might meet someone I knew. We walked along the streets on our way to the man who so greatly loved literature. My chief took my elbow and laid out his plan of action. First, he would put a few simple questions connected, naturally, with literature. Not literature in general, but in the narrow sense of the word. I was not to break in on their talk unless directly addressed, one careless word could spoil everything "Is that clear?" "Of course, of course." "Right. And don't look at the respondent all the time, he might be embarrassed or confused." "Embarrassed or confused?" I laughed bitterly. "If the world overturned, that one wouldn't turn a hair!" "Why not?" "I don't know." "That's interesting, too," remarked my chief. "Still, you'd better not stare at him." "I won't even give a glance." "No, no, nothing unnatural. No extremes, it's natural for you to glance at him now and then." "Very well, I'll send him a glance now and then," I promised. "And here we are." "Aha!" he gripped my arm above the elbow. "You know what,

Tamaz, I'll wait outside, and you tell him that a colleague, a little older and a step higher at work, would like to talk to him—if you do that, then be'll be favourably disposed, and I'll take up a position where I'll be visible from the studio. I'll walk up and down. Is that all clear?" Suddenly he changed his mind. "Although—no, we'll go in together."

IX

The man who loved literature was photographing a lady in a very low cut dress who was shivering with cold. "No, no, look up, up I said, still higher, now turn your head a very little to the left; don't tense up, don't be anxious, please, think of something pleasant, remember something really pleasant, your childhood, for instance, your carefree childhood, cast yourself back—no, not the back of the chair, in your thoughts, send them back some thirty years—er, twenty! Remember a happy childhood. Klim, quick with the cassette—your shoulders aren't cold? The cassette, Klim, put it in yourself, it's time you learned.... Oh, our Aureliano's here! Aureliano before he got fat! Good morning! I wasn't talking to you, ma'am, why did you nod, you've spoiled the pose, lift your head and open your eyes wider, raise your lids—not like that, you don't want to lock pop-eyed—yes, that's right don't look excited—no, now you're too Indifferent, have you stopped thinking about your happy childhood? Remember it, never mind it being a long time ago—you aren't cold? Splendid..."

He fussed about with the client for a long time, I thought he'd never finish. And when at last he did, everyone except myself got busy with something; the photographer felt in his pockets, slapped his sides, hunted through a drawer; Klim hurried to turn off the blinding light—let the lamp cool, and busied himself with the camera. "D'you know where my pencil is?" the photographer asked him. "No, it was in the drawer—" Meanwhile my chief approached the shivering woman and with a gallant smile held up her coat, raised it to the level of her naked shoulders, saying, "Please put this on, you'll catch cold." Before turning to slip her arms into the sleeves she gave him a momentary but all-encompassing glance and you could see even from the back of her head, even—imagine!—from her crisply curling hair that she was taken with him.... "Have you found it?" "No, Klim. How can I write out a receipt?" "Are you very cold?" my chief cooed, his voice was fascinating, beautiful, he was really enchanting. "N-no, not so very," she replied—she herself was quite attractive. "Have you looked in the drawer?" This, of course, was Klim. "Yes, it isn't there." "Where on earth can it have got to?" Klim, too, was bothered, while my chief was murmuring, "But you're warm now, aren't you?" The woman flushed. With a graceful movement of his middle finger he moved back the cuff of his elegant shirt and looked importantly as his watch; the woman, seizing her moment, sent him a look which, swift as it was, gave her an accurate picture of brows, lips and nose before she lowered her eyes again; he pleased her, very much he did; but the photographer was far from pleased at the disappearance of his pencil, he didn't know what to do. "There now, you've got warm, I can see by your neck," my chief continued. "You never ought to be cold, always warm," and all the time he was caressing her with his eyes. The woman sank her cheek into the fur of the collar as though evading his eyes but she certainly found him pleasing, very pleasing, if we hadn't been there I'm sure they would have been in each other's arms. "Perhaps Aureliano has a pen?" That was Klim. "Yes, that's it." said the photographer, but suddenly remembered, "No, his pen leaks. But perhaps his friend—" He nodded towards my chief who was now bending over the woman, smiling into her eves. "Er—excuse me but have you a pen?" But my chief was too much engaged to hear, and then that brisk Klim found the pencil in a book, our respondent wrote out the receipt and gave it to the client who now prepared to go, she tied a fluffy shawl round her head, my chief gallantly opened the door and helped her down two shallow steps, carefully holding her elbow. "Well—goodbye," and we remained four, two and two. But the photographer didn't know we had come together, he took my chief for a client. "Do you want a passport photo or—" "No, no," said my chief, smiling, "I've come with my—" "With Tamaz?" said the respondent in surprise and then it dawned. "Ah yes, you'll be his chief—young determined, energetic, the one who made such an excellent start?"

"Yes, that's right."

Suddenty the respondent cried out in amazement.

"Klim, is it my imagination, or is he really—"

"No, it isn't imagination."

"Extraordinary! Such a likeness! A real copy!"

"Wonderful!" Klim marvelled in his turn, slapping his side. "An amazing likeness!"

"I? Who is it I resemble?" My chief was embarrassed but did not show it and asked as though without any particular interest. "Some actor?"

"Eh? No, no." The respondent waved it off.

"Who, then?"

"A character in a book! You often get slight resemblances, but such a likeness! Unbelievable! Klim, he's the double of Giangiacomo Seminario, doesn't it catch your eye at once?"

"Of course it does. Like a twin brother!"

"Excuse me, but who might that individual be?" asked my chief, hanging on to the remnants of his self-control.

"The marshal's elder brother."

"What marshal, in heaven's name?"

"What—? Why, Betancourt, of course!" Then—imagine it—he pointed at me, and said solemly, "And do you know what your relationship to Tamaz would be if we went by that resemblance? His grandfather!"

"Just—*what* do vou mean?"

"Giangiacomo came from Ariadna Carrasco, isn't that right?" he said, calling Klim to aid his memory.

"Who is this Giangiacomo and marshal and all the rest of it?" My chief was now thoroughly tangled.

Embarrassment, floundering—indescribable. We were all staring awkwardly at each other

"A—ah I understand," at last said the man who loved literature. "You haven't read about Betancourt, that's it. You haven't, have you?"

"No—o," he answered, recovering a little, "Why deceive you? It's—some book?"

"Some book—and what a book! And you probably haven't read of Llosa, Mario Vargas..."

"Er—no."

"And Cortazar?"

"M-mm—no."

Suddenly the respondent seized his hand and shook it energetically.

"I congratulate you, I do, you're happy man—"

"Why?" asked my bewildered chief.

"Because a tremendous pleasure still ahead of you."

"Pleasure—?"

"The pleasure of reading it for the first time!"

But at this point, my chief remembered his future work; he threw back his head bending it slightly sideways, assumed a stern, businesslike expression, sat down, and drumming with his fingers on the glass—topped table, said formally, "Permit me to put a few questions to you."

"Of course, certainly," the respondent gave him a searching look and turned to Klim. "Hang this up so that we shan't be disturbed." "This" was a square piece of cardboard bearing the word in Georgian and Russian: "Closed."

X

The business was only now beginning, previously it had been preliminary fencing.

My chief and the eccentric respondent were sitting opposite one another, with Klim and myself like seconds. Everything was prepared—pen in hand, questionnaire unfolded, with the respondent all attention, my chief studied him, narrow-eyed, without any hurry; Klim was looking at the stranger doubtfully while I was eyeing the respondent with mistrust. Two against two.

My chief started.

"The most important, the essential function of the given questionnaire cannot be implemented on the basis of traditional questions, presupposing a calculation of the conditions of living and life in general. Consequently, they must be replaced by indices of the urbanisation of the surrounding—"

"Please ask your questions," the respondent interrupted.

"About what?" He sounded a bit irritated, he can't stand being interrupted. "In the first place you aren't aware of what I want to know."

"I didn't say I was aware—although as a matter of fact I am. If I'm not mistaken you intend to make a study of my leisure time and my way of life with the purpose of future improvements, isn't that so?"

"You want me to put my questions without any introduction or preparation?"

"Of course, Tamaz has done all the preparation. I even know that I'm the respondent and you're the interviewer."

"Very good," said my chief, smiling coldly. "So you are fond of literature, of fiction?"

"I don't deny it. I'm very fond of it."

"Splendid. What about newspapers and magazines."

"I must remark here that 'newspapers and magazines' is a senseless combination of words," said the respondent, vexed. "Magazines are one thing, newspapers are quite another. It beats me how they are always linked together, almost merged."

"M'yes. Which writers do you like?"

"What time is it, Klim?" the respondent asked suddenly.

"A quarter to four."

"Oh, then we shan't have time to go through them all, we only work till five."

My chief looked at me, frowning. He turned back to the respondent.

"What do you do if you're in a library and see somebody tearing a book?"

We expected some answer like "Strangle him, tear him to pieces," but the respondent answered indifferently, "Depends on what book it is."

That was unexpected and we didn't quite know how to react, but Klim cried admiringly, "Oh, splendid, maestro, wonderful!"

"Do you live alone?"

"No, there are two of us, myself and my brother. Grisha Kezheradze. We have a third brother. He's something very special, better than either Grisha or me, but he doesn't live with us, he walks about the villages. If Grisha and I—how shall I put it?—if Grisha and I could be called short stories, he'd be a whole novel."

"The one who lives with you, is he a literature enthusiast like you?"

"Who, Grisha? No. He likes reading all right, naturally, but not as I do, no! O—oh, he had his own problems, his enthusiasms, but he went to extremes, he'd talk to anybody and everybody about his problems, but then he decided to be tight-lipped. Says nothing and tunes pianos. He's a piano—tuner."

My chief sent me a second frowning look.

Nevertheless he continued, speaking as usual expressively, convincingly.

"You are fond of literature and that is excellent, reading is one of the purposeful forms of the cultural employment of time—*one* of the forms, I repeat; but what have you against, say, the graphic arts, what is wrong with a walk in the fresh air, or with beautiful music written by famous composers?...Yes, why don't you go dancing, or devote some time to the radio and television with their programmes, so rich in content, on the most widely divergent themes? Why don't you take up sport, or chess, or read good books—" He caught himself up, "oh yes, of course, you do read, well, then chess, it's an excellent game, and in general—"

He stopped. We waited.

"Please continue, continue," Klim suddenly broke in—Klim, actually telling my chief what to do! The impudence of it! Not even a proper man—a wretched, shabby newt of a creature, a mere nothing.

Then my indignant chief put his most difficult, most dynamic question, he was again his decided, unbending, purposeful self.

"Tell me, how would you organise life if it was in your power to do so?"

"Mine? My own life"

"No, my good man, the whole of society," he pronounced.

"Heavens above!" burst from the respondent. "Have I heard aright? That's the question I've been waiting for all my life!"

"Really?" He was struck with surprise. "You've thought about it, then?"

"It's the one thing I've given thought to," he said musingly, then livened up. "You want to know how I would organise life?" He walked about, looking at the photographs on the walls, most of the ladies in very low dresses wore serious expressions, probably to counter the the impression of nakedness, whereas those with high collars melted in smiles; of course there were exceptions, *décolleté* but smiling, and some women's faces had assumed a look of tragedy; the man whose picture had three times been blackened the previous day was in a prominent place, near it was a young man with an unpleasant smirk, likewise placed to catch the eye, and a little lower an obviously scoundrelly type; beside him a thin—lipped man looked suspiciously in his direction. There were pleasant faces, too, a laughing child... "How would I organise things?" The respondent livened up. "I'd build a whole town of cells."

"What?" My chief was thunderstruck. "How would—I mean—you want a tyranny?"

"Good Lord, no, heaven forbid!" The respondent smiled reassuringly. "They wouldn't be cells in the ordinary meaning of the word, they would be luxury cells."

"Luxury cells?"

"Your surprise is natural," the respondent agreed. "There are words which can be combined only with difficulty, and those two 'luxury' and 'cell', are among them, yet there are no two words which can never be linked, and 'luxury cell' is a case in point—a luxury cell with a multitude of books, with a comfortable upholstered armchair and a reading lamp standing on a small, handsome table—in a word, a cell any book—lover might dream of. After all, not everyone can read with enjoyment in a library reading room. To one who voluntarily, on his own two legs, enters the place, I have designed it will be simply luxury, but to many it would be a luxury cell.... I really should have begun with that. Say, you have a bunch of lads, larrikins, standing propping up a wall in some street, talking tough, spitting, going nowhere in particular, not thinking about time because they haven't anything special to do so it's all the same to them what time it is, or whether it's day or night, they jostle girls, let out wolf whistles, impudent jokes—amuse themselves in their own way, exchanging occasional kicks, grinning—and suddenly we appear, I and others of my kind, grab them and into these luxury cells with them."

"By force?" asked my chief and wrote something for the first time.

"Yes, by force," the respondent said firmly. "It may be necessary even to twist their arms. You know—there are some who put their faith in family influence, others rely on school, a third will base his hopes on some organisation or the moral force of the community, some think the best method is a good beating—and God alone knows what else, but I consider my luxury cell the best, the one thing that will save them. We take our young ne'er—do—well and put him in a luxury cell—alone, naturally. He looks about him wildly—barred window, locked door. It is guarded outside by some Klim, sitting reading. Our young fellow looks round at the table, chair and bookshelves without any interest, he goes unhurriedly to the clean bed, stretches himself out on it, again examines everything about him; after a while his eyes dull and he falls asleep. His parents have already been informed, of course: 'Don't be anxious, please, your son is confined in a luxury cell.' 'That's good, my dear fellow, very good, if only it stops him hanging about the streets, if he finds better use for his time, and then—' The young man wakes, stares dully at the ceiling, and then discovers that he's hungry. 'What shall I bring you?' asks some Klim through the door. 'Tea, coffee, cocoa?' 'Cocoa, but why am I locked up?' But that Klim doesn't answer his question. 'How much sugar?' 'Four spoonfuls, and why am I locked up?' But that Klim only says: 'What kind of cheese—Imeritin, suluguni?' 'Suluguni, but why have they locked me up?' But that Klim silently holds out his breakfast. The young fellow butters his bread, peels an egg and is occupied for some time with eating. 'Would you like some cigarettes?' 'Yes, that would be good.' 'Mziuri, Colchis, Lux?' All right, but there is nothing that can amuse him, this room isn't only 'luxury', but also a cell. So he smokes and stares at the ceiling. And on the ceiling there is an alphabet—A B C D and so on. A good idea, eh, Klim?"

What did Klim say? "Excellent," of course.

"Dinner-time comes—first course, second, sweet. 'Will you take your salad with sunflower oil, vinegar or without anything?' 'Why have I been shut up, why?' He is told, 'None of your business.' If he starts to shout and stamp and wave his fists you have to say, 'Now, now' and 'tut-tut' and he'll calm down and eat his dinner. After dinner he'll start staring at the ceiling again with its letters, and then that Klim will say very casually, 'You could leaf through one of the books on that shelf.' So the young fellow will take a book, at first it will be a book for small children with large print and colourful pictures; if he takes to them willingly, good, if not, the Klim assigned to him will tell him, 'You'll stop here until you've read all the books in the bookcase and on the shelves.'"

"But that's coercion!" said my chief. "Some concrete person should on his own initiative select one or another of social means of..."

"At present I am talking about idle youths, dear sir," the respondent explained. "What right would I have to seize some chemist, for instance, and place him—" he stopped and thought deeply for a moment, them concluded, "Although it would do no harm to a chemist lacking general education, damn it...?"

XI

"H'm!" My chief's nerves were on edge, he didn't quite know how to handle this; he passed his hand over his cheek and chin—were they well shaven?—and his eye fell on Klim. "Very well, but what has that Klim-fellow done, to have to spend the whole day guarding this idler and listening to his complaints?"

"In the first place, I mentioned an open book on his knees. and secondly, he can always find some harmless amusement."

"For instance?"

"A word game, for instance."

"Word?"

"I'll explain. Take our Tamaz. What's his job called?"

"Junior scientific employee."

"Good. And what was he before that?"

"Laboratory assistant."

"And you promoted him?"

"Yes."

"Aha! So in this case 'junior' meant a rise?"

"Quite right."

"So you can get a fine word, you 'juniorscienced' him."

For the third time my chief gave me a frowning look.

"Now let's take it the opposite way—say, Tamaz is reduced to laboratory assistant. How would he express that himself?"

"I become laboratory assistant," my chief answered for me.

"No, no good, the demotion isn't expressed.

"Demoted me to laboratory assistant."

"Shorter."

"Made me lab assistant."

"Still shorter."

"Demotion."

"But where's the laboratory assistant? Find one word to express both demotion and position."

"One word? Impossible."

"Why?"

"Very well, try jourself if it's so easy."

"Labdowngraded. See? So this Klim-chappie could amuse himself with words."

"Bravo, maestro! Wonderful!" That was Klim, of course.

Ah, chief, chief!

A fourth frowning look in my direction.

Silence. Klim was looking at the respondent with delighted admiration, the respondent was absorbed in thoughts of his own, my chief likewise, I alone didn't know what to do, I fidgeted with my tie as I repeated to myself that hideous word, "labdowngraded." We had to stumble on just this man! Why couldn't I have passed his place by? But who could guess—? Now it was too late. My chief was interested; actually, I fancy he rather regretted having come, but all the same he continued—determined, energetic.

"How do you select the literature?"

"To start with—anything you like, everyone could choose for himself—something easy, say, Simenon or bound copies of our magazine *Crocodile or Niangi,* but probably best of all, something by Jules Verne. The important thing is to get used to sitting at a table with a book—stretching your legs out comfortably or crossing your feet under the table, learning to leaf through a book, getting an idea of what it's about, and when we've got so far, then offer him-well, Klim?—Yes. *The Three Musqueteers*, or Mark Twain—although personally, for the life of me I can't get to like him—or O. Henry, and then introduce him to the more serious writers—Klim, give me two. Excellent—Jack London and of course Victor Hugo's prose, called romantic and not at all easy reading; then we'll give him a little rest—*The Headless Horseman* and *Ivanhoe*, for instance. And after that, Klim, let's arrange his happy meeting with those great writers who are so easy to read—yes, Prosper Mérimée, Chekhov—one more? Quite right, quite right, we'll give him Mérimée, Chekhov and Maupassant; then it'll be time to risk it, give him something more complex, only not that novel, he's not got so far, Klim. He's not up to *Death in Venice* yet, what are you thinking of, lad. Something after that style but more within his reach, comparatively easy—comparatively, I said, and a wee bit old-fashioned—well, Dickens, maybe!"

"Dickens, good, splendid," cried my chief. *"David Copperfield!"*

"You think so?" The respondent sounded ironical but my chief, pleased with himself, didn't notice.

"Of course. It is delightful to sit sometimes in the shade reading Dickens."

"Sometimes Dickens in the shade, and maybe sometimes even Tolstoy?" Klim, that pigwidgin, that snivelling runt, was actually making a mock of my chief, but the respondent took up the theme.

"No point in continuing the list, these will do for the present. Now we must look at the young fellow, observe his expression as he reads. If he is sufficiently caught up by what he's reading, we can let him go."

"But how can you tell whether he's caught up or not?"

"By his expression."

"Well, and what'll be the result?"

"For whom?"

"Your young fellow."

Solemnly the respondent pronounced: "The result will be another Klim."

There was a moment's silence, and then my chief stubbornly continued.

"So then—what? What will emerge from it all?"

"What should emerge, my dear fellow—a person who is very fond of literature will emerge."

"Literature, pah! The most important thing in the world!" My chief was thoroughly irritated.

"*What! What!*" The respondent was thunderstruck. "Is it really necessary to explain it?!"

"Try. I'm all attention!"

"Try?" The respondent thought a moment, looking him in the eye. "Try? In that case, I'll start by explaining it in a simple way, one you'll understand: after reading any good book you'll become just a little better, a little wiser than you were, and incidentally—" his face brightened—"I am increasingly convinced that good sense is something very necessary." His face became sterner. "That, as I said, is a simple, primitive explanation, but quite sufficient—you become better. Now I'll try to go into it more deeply."

He began to pace the room.

Backwards and forwards.

Silence.

XII

"Of all the sounds on earth," the respondent began with quiet restraint, "I would choose one as the most dreadful, sorrowful, unbearable, heart-shaking and I can't say what more the thud of clods on the top of a lowered coffin—you remember? Yes. Dull, dead thuds. But even without that, without so much as remembering it, you suddenly wake in the dead of night, in the darkness—in an instant you come from sleep to wakefulness and with hideous clarity remember about death which will some day come, never doubt it. That is the one thing that you know with certainty, which you can never doubt; nevertheless, in the daytime the sunshine, among other people—ho-ho-ho, as lively and cheerful as yourself, you wash with loud snorting, you have breakfast—chew your ham as strongly as though it were made of iron, leave the house, meet each other, one senior, another junior, but none exactly equal—that's among your own kind, the great majority whom we count among the ones 'to be congratulated', you know now whom we mean—those who still have before them the great happiness of a first reading; well, but what separates myself and Klim? Regard me as the chief of a photography studio and him as a junior assistant, still we are equal, the same, because both of us are devoted to literature, and unlike you, 'those-to-be-congratulted', we don't want to climb or advance, and we fear death much less than others because we have already died many times and experienced everything—yes, we have been knights and kings, we have fought with wooden swords in a good cause, we have worn crowns of laurels and crowns of thorns, soft carpets have been spread before our feet and flowers strewn before us, but we have also been made to tread burning coals barefoot; we have chattered, talked nonsense in leisure hours but we have also known what it is to preserve silence, clenching our teeth, guarding the secrets of others; but that sound, that thud—that sound reaches us all the same. We would wish to live many lives, various lives, and we, bent over books in our rooms—what deaths have we not known—we have drowned in the sea, fallen in battle, mounted the scaffold, and died quietly in our beds after escaping many dangers, died surrounded alongside the gallant cat-eyed El Sordo, and have ourselves killed others and later repented, oh, how we repented! We have kissed the earth, and crumbs of that sacred soil have clung to our lips, we have risen to seek vengeance, we have wandered, following winding paths, we have been wetted by rains—many rains, but I think, Klim, the best rain of all was Bunin's and then his snow falling lightly and sadly, and the ice—smooth, gleaming, slippery! But all the same those dull thuds were heard, they echoed in your ears. With the first vague light we leave the house, the people walking along the streets in the early morning are strange, sleepy, but in their crumpled, dull faces there is some vague desire, some vague, hidden strength, and hope wakens with somebody's 'Good morning' and you wander alone, without reason or aim, because you are in love with everything, and although you love people so boundlessly, yet sometimes you want to be alone with yourself, and remember that you can still walk about outside the town, that there is still the thick forest and deep caves where you can crouch for a long time in the dimness and damp, and then, emerging into the light, blink in the sunshine and, born anew, tell yourself the world is great and beautiful. Ah man, man, you are an ocean, an ocean, filled with supple fish, now furiously fighting the storm, now calm and peaceful, but in your depths thought moves lazily like the fronds of seaweed. You are an ocean basking in the sunshine, but at night, waking suddenly, you think again and again about death and feel that you are gradually evaporating, and in the end you will evaporate completely, dry up, and your fish too will lie dead. But however great your despair, your depression, your stubborn fish nevertheless need food, and we again hurry about the world, the great blessed world and, Lord God Almighty, what haven't we experienced! Leaving all else aside, how many times we have fallen in love! What are Marania and Tenorio compared to us, we are the real Don Juans, myself and some Klim. Don Juan readers. Whom have we not loved—a living buoyant Natasha, loved to distraction in the first three volumes and in the fourth-what's to be done?—we cooled to her and loved Sonechka, holy, pure and slandered, and Tonka, quiet, irresponsible, distant, but nevertheless so close, so close, until... Aime Tanatogenos with such pain, and even that sinful Madame Bovary. Antonia, my poor Antonia I love especially, with sharp torment, and Selina dancing in the smoke. Clawdia, the proud mistress of Chauchat, and Pilar, Pilar Ternera in thick darkness smelling of smoke, and Maya, the Khevsur, Maya Chincharauli—ah, not only I, the very walls, stairs, the things about her adored her, and who can say how many more! Where have I not been, what places have I not visited! With curved knives, with machetes I have slashed thorny scrub, I have pursued the white foe in the ocean and it seems loved him, I have dreamed of mountain heights and what attempts have followed! A cat, they say, has nine lives, but how many lives have I had through loving all this! But you, interviewers, recipients of congratulations, are concerned with such questions as 'how long must I queue for vermicelli' when in those same minutes you can wander to unknown imagined places, Sight is a great gift but fantasy, with its hundred eyes and hundred ears, is far beyond, and it is hard to say who was really in Peru or Nigeria—I, or some pilot smoking his pipe who has roamed the world."

"How do you come to know about Nigeria?" My chief was not beating any retreat, he was ready to catch the respondent. But the respondent was not perturbed.

"Nigeria, my dear man, has three excellent writers—Soyinka, Chinua Achebe and Gabrièl Okara."

No, it was impossible to talk to him, and although my chief no longer frowned at me and even avoided my eye. I was conscious that inwardly he was seething and again remembered that horrible word "labdowngraded", while the man who loved literature continued.

"To be a reader is a miracle in itself, a reader can, for instance, lie between two lovers in an already tight sleeping bag and not be in the way, it's not only a miracle, I'll say more, he can be necessary because the author so willed it."

"Why 'willed it'?"

"Because it was necessary." And continued:

XIII

"It seems to me there is something in common between wine and books. Both give the sensation of what is often called a liberated personality. But in the one case this liberation is something unruly, ugly, degrading, born of irresponsibility, in the other it is elevated and elevating, all-powerful—you understand? Oh, with what satisfaction I would shut a drunkard up in my luxury cell, and follow him with those big business tycoons—not the petty swindlers but the masters of really big machinations—do you know why? You can't imagine how I fool for them! Don't ever think of them as fortunate or happy, my friend, and most important, don't envy them—however good a show they may put up, whatever they may pretend to themselves and others, nevertheless each of their days is poisoned and darkened because there is that instant before falling asleep, that fleeting instant when we all see ourselves as we are without any false colouring. Don't envy them the luxurious food which they have in abundance because when they have thoroughly filled their stomachs they feel an incomprehensible wish for something more, and they don't realise that this need is for the plain food of the poor man—bread and an onion! We readers do not envy their riches because *Don Quixote* is more real than all their rings and all their well-filled cupboards. And by the way, physicists will never create perpetual motion, but literature has already created what is eternal—*Don Quixote*. Well, so we'll shut up all these tycoons in luxury cells and make them start with the alphabet—of course they are literate, but the whole essence of the method is the sequence—and keep them shut up until Pshavela's *Tale of a Goat* no longer sets them thinking of *shashlyk* but of something much more important and necessary."

"In the first place," said my chief, already exasperated, "how can you tell which writer is great and which is not? That's something which it sometimes takes centuries to decide."

"That's a very good question, and your interest is perfectly natural. I'll explain. What shall we begin with? Say what you will, there do exist weak, petty writers with their lifeless, faceless characters whom we need no more than-Klim, suggest a comparison, a fruity one—eh, Klim, that's fruity all right! Well, of course among writers just like others you get those who hunt easy game which they grab easily and which has a valuable skin, but if you're a real reader you know what's what, because there are also the bold writers who can with amazing calm take risks with no thought of themselves—like trainers who put their heads in a lion's mouth—not in the same category as those who make a curly little dog with a bow on its neck jump through a hoop, but real tamers able to subdue a wolf—a beast which can never be trained, and to catch its tail but for an instant is far harder than to put your head in a lion's mouth! And what if sometimes when you fight the wolf you are ragged as a beggar while the trainer of little dogs is tricked out in all the grandeur of a hussar? If you wish to know my ideal writer I can tell you, it is the proud ragamuffin riding the wolf with an eagle on his shoulder, although they say an eagle too cannot be tamed.... And I will say, finally, that the great writer is he who can create great books—"

"Yes, and secondly," my chief interrupted again, "how can you be sure which books are great and which not?"

"I have, my dear sir, my own determining indicator, more reliable than the finest of instruments. If I read something really significant, a book or even a metaphor from it—if, I say again, it is really significant, I get gooseflesh. You don't believe it?" The respondent rolled his sleeve and pronouncing the words *"Don Quixote"* showed us his arm and—there's no denying it—there it was, gooseflesh.

But my chief wasn't beaten, he at once came up with a new question.

"I cannot understand what principle you follow in naming the writers and the women you allegedly love: do you follow some chronological principle, or alphabetic—or what?"

"Lord above! You hear what he's saying, Klim?!" The respondent clapped his palm loudly to his forehead. "What can they have in common—from whence and whither—love, and the alphabet! My sainted aunt! Here's one to be congratulated a dozen times, Klim! A rare example!"

"Congratulation isn't enough, he should be tossed like an Olympic champion!" cried Klim.

"May I request a little more courtesy." My chief was really angry now. "What's the sense of pestering me with your damned literature? I can use the same tactics. What do you know about my science and its famous people? Who were Emil Durkheim and Max Weber, or Parsons and Merton? How much have you heard about Pareto and von Wiese—" My chief was infuriated and I rejoiced. "Who were Szczepanski, Becker and Pitirim Sorokin?"

"Well then, we'll leave literature," said the respondent. "You have forgotten that I'm not a littérateur but a photographer, and I can equally well match your names with those of the leading men in photography. What have you heard, for instance, about the great Louis Daguerre, what can you say about the achievements of Carl Zeiss and Joffe, what are the links between photography and polygraphy, and what was invented by Ernst Leitz? What should be the exposure in weather like the present, for instance, and what do you think of Max Alpert? Which works by Rodchenko, Mikulin and Tikanadze do you like best?" A pause, then slyly. "Well?"

I received a fifth frown from my chief.

What a horrible, hideous word that is—"labdowngraded"!

"But all the same, all the same, I have to confess," and the respondent looked sadly at my chief, "I've no faith in the possibility of setting up my luxury cells—not because it isn't worth while, no. And it isn't true that you cease to fear death if you've seen a lot and experienced a lot—on the contrary, it makes it even harder to part with life, but you will at least know that you have lived fully and seen the whole world. And a man like myself may perhaps say on his deathbed, 'Eh, but It was good, damn it—' while a man like you, in blooming health, may ask, gloating, 'What—life or literature?' But I—would you like to know what I will answer to that?"

"What?" My chief asked, evidently losing his confidence.

"I will answer: 'Wasn't it the same thing?'"

"Splendid, maestro!" ejaculated Klim, and the respondent continued.

"I have tried not to show you, the ones to be congratulated, the full measure of my superiority and have said not a went about poetry; I spared you, because our little Georgia is one of the greatest and mightiest lands on the poetie map of the world."

"Poetry, poetry, just Imagine how important that is!" My chief's face abowed red patches.

"'A child fell in the street down in the dusty street,'" whispered the respondent. "What can be more heart-breaking than that—you are struck by the power of poetry."

"He fell—what a tragedy!" said my chief contemptuously.

"So he fell down, and then somebody of course picked him up! Which of us never fell when we were small, and with the assistance of meritorious persons were restored unharmed to our feet. What is there to rave about?"

"Lord above, listen to him carrying on!" The respondent flung up his hands. "Did you hear that, Klim? Like a savage!" Excitedly he asked, "Could you repeat it?"

"Why not?" My chief wasn't retreating, he was unbending as always.

"Klim! I implore you—run to number twenty-three, to Vanno, if he isn't home then here's my passport, borrow a tape recorder for ten minutes, we'll record that sentence and return it at once! Run, Klim, here, take the passport." He was wildly excited yet seemed to be half joking. "A tape recorder! Half my kingdom for a tape recorder! Klim! How did he put it—'With the assistance of meritorious persons.' Quick, Klim, fly!"

"Don't waste your effort," said my chief, his voice shaking. "We're going."

He rose, I rose and we moved towards the door; we straightened our ties, put on our coats while the respondent—jacket-less in his shirt-sleeves, asked us to stay, begged us: but my chief remained adamant, he reached out decisively towards the door handle and for the sixth time gave me a frowning look. The respondent—the insolence of it!—offered to photograph us. "Please, I beg you—for my collection—it will be the photograph of the century, on one picture together, Colonel Giangiacomo Seminario and Aureliano the Fat before he became fat!"

But my furious chief roughly pushed the respondent aside. Then the latter directed his big tripod camera on us, and ran to the table for a plate, but my chief shouted, "We don't want to be photographed, you hear me? We don't want it!" and with fingers like iron claws pushed his hand away. The photographer's face jerked with pain, the plate fell down, and we both—first my chief and then I—left the place. The respondent followed us with a camera, not the big one, one of the smaller makes, and aimed it at us. My chief raised his collar and hid his face while I stood, lost and confused; at any moment now I would start to yawn. My chief went to a brick wall and almost pressed his face against it. He stood there, with one hand pulling his collar over his face, and putting on his dark glasses with the other, and the photographer called Klim. He, of course, was there at once, the other gave him the camera and grasped my chief's shoulder, strong and energetic as he was, meaning to turn him round—imagine it! I was amazed, why didn't my chief, a real athlete, and angry, infuriated in fact, give him a good punch in the face, but in the same instant I realised that he couldn't punch his nose in the street, in broad daylight, however great his fury, because that would be a street brawl, and who starts a brawl! And although the street is narrow and quiet, a few people had already stopped to look and others had their heads out of windows to take in the show: 1) an athlete in dark glasses hiding his face against a brick wall with raised arms, 2) a man in shirt-sleeves—in winter!—holding his sleeve, 3) myself, yawning Indifferently from excitement, and 4) little Klim, holding a camera, on one knee in the middle of the road! Of course, people took us for hooligans, bandits or at the very least people causing traffic trouble—who else would be forcibly photographed in the middle of the street! Klim was waiting stubbornly, half squatting, but my chief found a way. Stepping sideways, not leaving the wall, not turning his face from it, he moved towards our offices, and out of respect I too followed him sideways; but suddenly we heard a terrible, grievous wail from the respondent, "Oh heavens, Klim's been run over by a car!"

We turned sharply, shocked, and before we could take it in Klim jumped to his feet—car? There was no car—and carefully closed the camera which a split second before had given a "click" hideous to us but desired by them. Then the man who loved literature and his assistant Klim, just a little embarrassed at having got their way, ran off and vanished.

And it had all started with my chief sending for me and saying. "Our investigations shall concern firstly the leisure occupations of inhabitants of settlements of an urban type which is one of the factors determining personality, and is a compenent part of the type of life and behaviour; secondly, investigations of that kind enable us..."

Labdowngraded...

Translated by Eve Manning

More Cuppa Classics

Why I Am an Atheist
Bhagat Singh
ISBN: 978-93-92210-45-7

The Republic
Plato
ISBN: 978-93-49042-15-5

The Idiot
Fyodor Dostoevsky
ISBN: 978-93-49042-49-0

The Great Gatsby
F Scott Fitzgerald
ISBN: 978-93-49042-81-0

The Art of War
Sun Tzu
ISBN: 978-93-92210-79-2

Moby Dick
Herman Melville
ISBN: 978-93-49042-86-5

The Trial
Franz Kafka
ISBN: 978-93-49042-88-9

The Story of My Life
Helen Keller
ISBN: 978-93-49042-32-2

The Adventures of Tom Sawyer
Mark Twain
ISBN: 978-93-49042-82-7

Adventures of Huckleberry Finn
Mark Twain
ISBN: 978-93-49042-59-9

Steppenwolf
Herman Hesse
ISBN: 978-93-49042-07-0

A Farewell to Arms
Ernest Hemingway
ISBN: 978-93-49042-76-6

For More Cuppa Classics